The Copycat

Kathleen and Donald Hersom
illustrated by Catherine Stock

S I M O N & S C H U S T E R

LONDON • SYDNEY • NEW YORK • TOKYO • SINGAPORE • TORONTO

I have a cat, a bold copycat, who lurks in the cow shed to moo at the cow,

And sprawls in the pigsty
and grunts at the sow.

I have a cat, a bold copycat,
who floats on the duck pond
and quacks at the drakes,

And slides through the heather
to hiss at the snakes.

I have a cat, a bold copycat,
who sleeps in a kennel
and barks at the dog,

And jumps in the water
to croak at the frog.

I have a cat, a bold copycat,
who flits to and fro
in the dusk with the bats,

And scuttles and squeaks
in the barn with the rats.

I have a cat, a bold copycat, who clucks in the farmyard and pecks at the fowls,

And startles the graveyard, outscreeching the owls.

IN MEMORY OF
FRED HARRIES

I have a cat, a bold copycat,
who trots to the stable
and neighs at the mare,

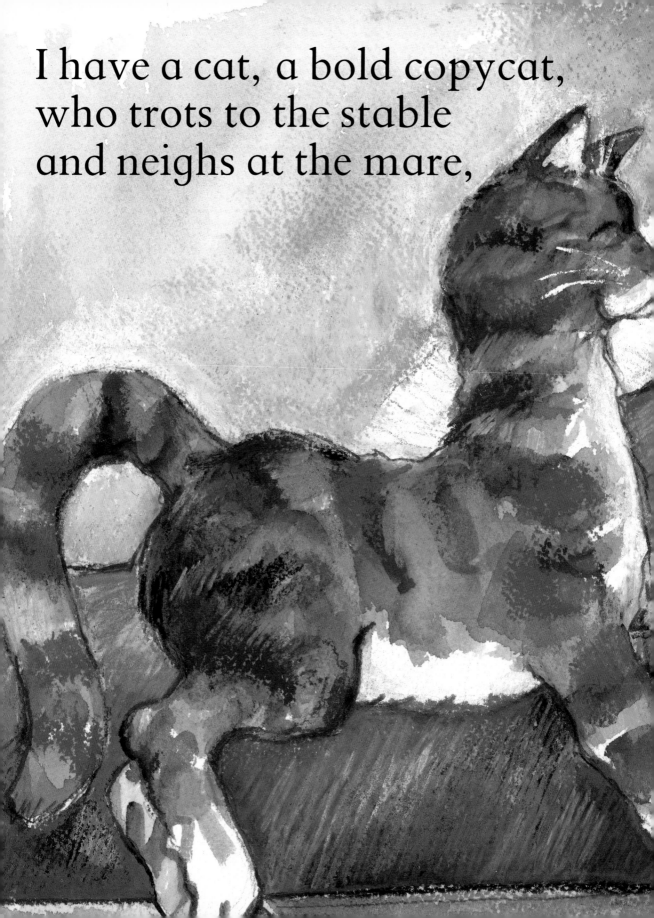

Who leaps up the hillside
to dance with the hare,

And copycats me
when I cuddle my bear!

Do you have a cat,
a stay-at-home cat,
who would sit
on a mat . . .

And teach
Meow!
to my cat?

To Natalie, Timothy,
Steadman, Wendy, Matthew, Herman,
Ellen, and Tony, with love – K.H. and D.H.

For Elaine – C.S.

First published in Great Britain in 1990 by
Simon & Schuster Young Books, Simon & Schuster International Group
Wolsey House, Wolsey Road, Hemel Hempstead, Herts. HP2 4SS

First published in the USA in 1989 by Atheneum, Macmillan Publishing Company

Typeset in 34pt Bembo educational by Goodfellow & Egan Ltd., Cambridge
Printed and bound in Belgium by Proost International Book Production

British Library Cataloguing in Publication Data
Hersom, Kathleen and Donald
The Copycat
I. Title II. Hersom, Donald III. Stock, Catherine
823. '914 [J]

ISBN 0-7500-0421-5
ISBN 0-7500-0422-3 pbk